What about Emma?

written and illustrated by Ken Rush

ORCHARD BOOKS   New York

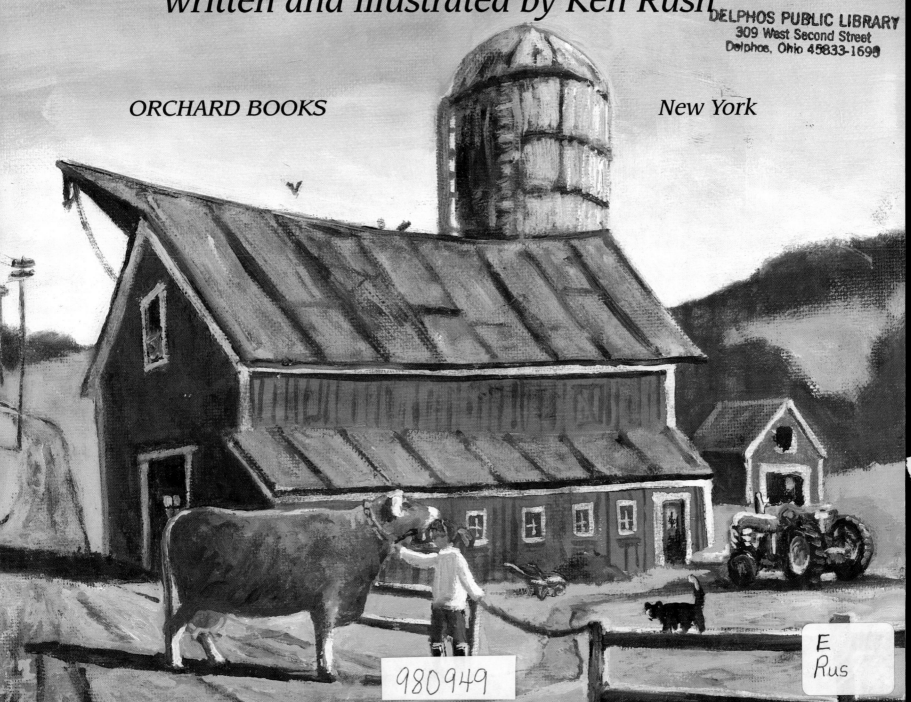

Orchard Books, 95 Madison Avenue, New York, NY 10016

Manufactured in the United States of America. Printed by Barton Press, Inc. Bound by Horowitz/Rae.
Book design by Jean Krulis. The text of this book is set in 14 point Leawood Medium. The illustrations
are oil on canvas reproduced in full color.

1   3   5   7   9   10   8   6   4   2

Library of Congress Cataloging-in-Publication Data
Rush, Ken. What about Emma? / written and illustrated by Ken Rush. p.   cm. Summary: Sue's family
is quitting the dairy business, so they sell all the cows except Emma, Sue's favorite, because she is
going to have a calf soon. ISBN 0-531-09534-7.—ISBN 0-531-08884-7 (lib. bdg.) [1. Farm life—
Fiction. 2. Cows—Fiction.] I. Title.
PZ7.R8954Wh   1996   [E]—dc20   95-53730

This book could not have happened without the kind help provided by the Vermont farming families of Bill and Lauren Downey, Don and Sue Mellen, George and Joyce Raymond, and Truman Young, Jr.

This book is dedicated to them, and to family farmers everywhere.

Our cow barn is old and red and really big. I like to watch the cows line up at milking time. As soon as my dad opens the gate, they file right into the barn. I get to hitch Emma up to the milking machine. Emma's my favorite cow. She's a big Brown Swiss who's going to calve this winter.

I squirt my brother, Pete, in the face with a shot of warm milk. "Gotcha!"

"Bull's-eye!" Pete laughs as he squirts me back.

For supper Mom serves up our favorite—chicken pie. Finally Dad puts down his napkin and looks straight at Pete and me. We get real quiet.

"I guess you kids know that times have been hard. Your mom and I have done about all we can to keep the farm going, but the price of feed and new equipment has gotten too high. Now, with the price of milk so low . . . well, we just can't afford to run a dairy farm anymore. I've taken a job down at the mill, and Mom's going to work more hours at the store."

"You mean we won't be milking?" Pete cries.

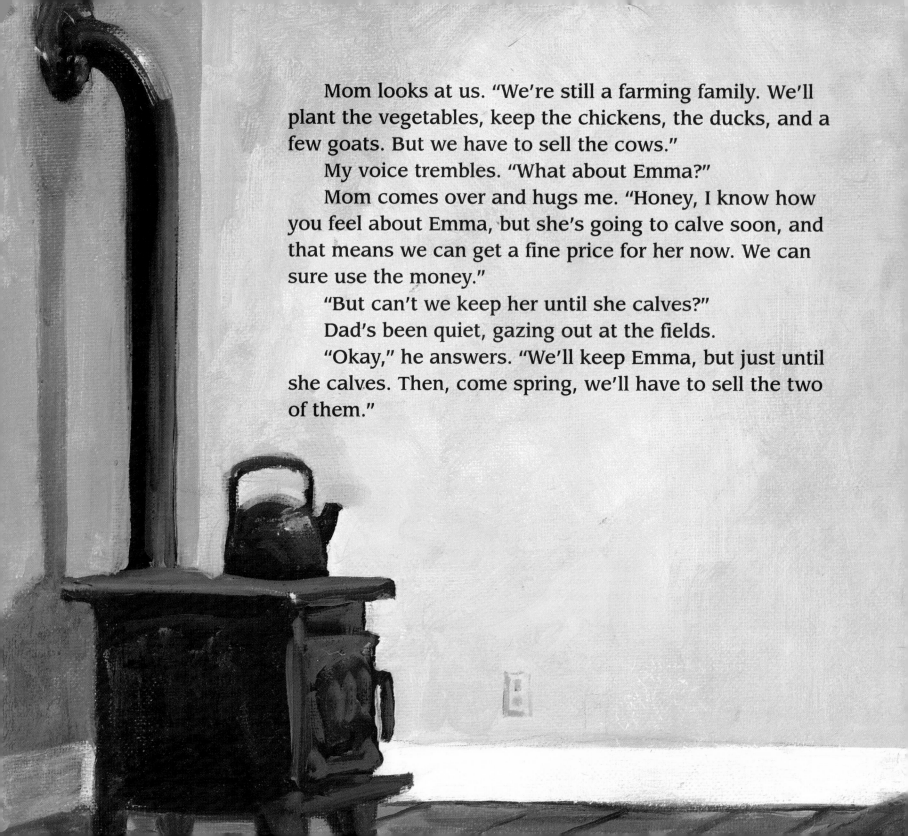

Mom looks at us. "We're still a farming family. We'll plant the vegetables, keep the chickens, the ducks, and a few goats. But we have to sell the cows."

My voice trembles. "What about Emma?"

Mom comes over and hugs me. "Honey, I know how you feel about Emma, but she's going to calve soon, and that means we can get a fine price for her now. We can sure use the money."

"But can't we keep her until she calves?"

Dad's been quiet, gazing out at the fields.

"Okay," he answers. "We'll keep Emma, but just until she calves. Then, come spring, we'll have to sell the two of them."

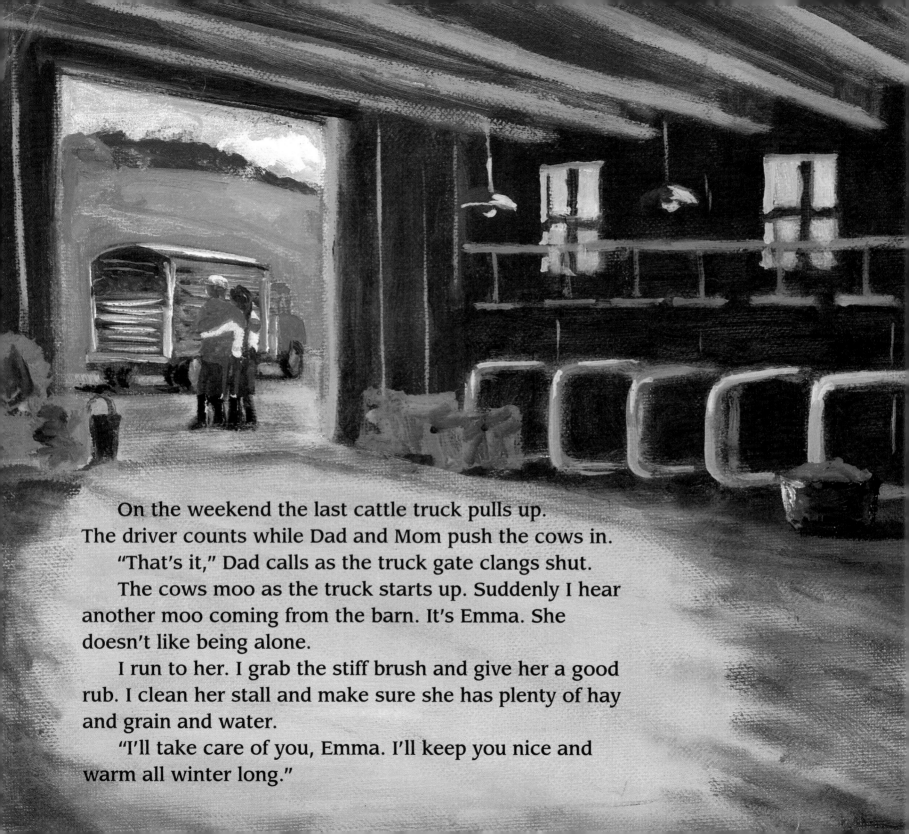

On the weekend the last cattle truck pulls up.
The driver counts while Dad and Mom push the cows in.

"That's it," Dad calls as the truck gate clangs shut.

The cows moo as the truck starts up. Suddenly I hear
another moo coming from the barn. It's Emma. She
doesn't like being alone.

I run to her. I grab the stiff brush and give her a good
rub. I clean her stall and make sure she has plenty of hay
and grain and water.

"I'll take care of you, Emma. I'll keep you nice and
warm all winter long."

After school Pete and I take Emma for a walk up in the woods.

"I'm gonna ride her," I announce.

"Cut it out. You can't even get on her."

I jump, and after a few tries I manage to pull myself up. It's hard to get balanced, but Emma doesn't mind.

"Giddyap, Emma." I pat her big neck, but she just stands there and swishes her tail.

After a week of practice, every time I climb on Emma and say "Giddyap," she starts right up and heads straight to the barn.

"Stop it, Sue," Pete scolds me. "You're turning that cow into a trail horse."

With the weather getting colder, I take shorter rides. It gets dark earlier now. Emma's belly is really big. She seems restless.

Dad comes in from work and looks Emma over real slow.

"When's she going to calve, Dad?" I ask.

"She's way past due now, and she's as broad as this old barn. We'll give her one more day, and then I'll have to call the vet. Make sure Emma's got lots of hay. We're in for a big snowstorm tonight."

We hurry to finish our chores. I take an extra bale of hay and spread it in Emma's stall.

After dinner we cozy up to the stove. We can see that the snow is coming down hard.

"I'm just remembering," Dad thinks aloud, "stormy nights like this we'd be checking, making sure that none of the herd wandered off in the snow. With just Emma, I guess we don't have much to check. Well, let's get to bed. We'll be shoveling out tomorrow for sure!"

Lying in bed, I listen to the whistle of the wind. Suddenly I hear a different sound. I hold my breath so I can hear better. There it is again, a deep bellow. It's Emma, and it sounds like something's wrong.

I tiptoe into Pete's room. "Wake up, Pete. Emma's calling."

We quietly creep downstairs and pull on our boots and jackets.

"Shouldn't we wake Mom and Dad?" I ask.

"Let's check her first," Pete whispers.

We struggle to the barn through the whirling snow, but even before we get to the stall we see the side door's blown open. Emma's gone!

"Where is she?"

"Look, Pete." I can barely see Emma through the snow. "She's heading for the woods!"

"We have to follow her or we'll lose her," Pete yells as we chase after her.

The woods are so dark that we can't find Emma.

"Emma, Emma," we call. Suddenly I hear her moo.

"There she is!" I yell. Sure enough, she's standing in a hollow, deep in snow. "Come, Emma, come, girl."

Emma won't budge. Pete tries to pull her with the hitching rope, but she just looks confused. "We've got to lead her to the barn," Pete yells over the wind. "She must be getting ready to calve."

"Help me up, Pete. I'll ride her out." He hesitates, but when he sees I mean it, he gives me a boost. "Come on, Emma." I pat her neck. "Giddyap, Emma, giddyap."

She slowly turns, takes a step forward, then stops. Emma's shaking so, and her back's so slick, that I can barely hold on.

"Giddyap, Emma, giddyap," I call. Suddenly she pulls out of the hollow and starts walking. She follows Pete out of the woods and down to the barn.

As we dry her off, Emma shudders and gives a bellow. "She's starting to calve," Pete shouts. "There's the hooves coming out and, look, there's the calf's nose. I'll get Mom and Dad."

Before I can answer, Dad's voice surprises us.

"What've we got here?" Dad calls as he and Mom enter the stall. He takes one look at Emma and says, "She's calving, all right, and it looks like she needs some help. Here, Sue, hold her tail aside." Dad grabs the calf's legs and starts to pull. Emma pushes, and the whole head of her calf is born. It's wet and glistening.

Emma bellows so loudly that I shut my eyes, and when I open them Emma's calf is lying beside her.

The newborn is shiny and wet, and Emma gets right to work. She licks and nudges her calf until it wobbles to its feet. Emma lows softly as the calf nurses.

"Would you look at that"—Mom laughs—"a beautiful new calf."

"So what are you going to name her?" Dad asks us.

I think for a minute. "Snowy," I answer, "because she was born in a snowstorm."

"Well." Dad pats Emma and runs his hand down Snowy's back. "Emma's warm and safe, and so's her calf. No sense losing any more sleep. We'll check the two of them in the morning. Let's get back to bed."

Pete gives me a good-natured shove as we all head back to the house.

The storm's quieted down, and my bed feels soft and warm. I can't hear Emma or her calf, but I know they're snug in the barn. Tomorrow I'll tell Mom and Dad about my ride. Then I'll ask if we can keep Emma and Snowy for good. I'll promise to take care of them, and I know Pete will too. They just might say yes.